W9-AVJ-770

Princess Justina Albertina

A Cautionary Tale

Ellen Dee Davidson

Illustrated by **Michael Chesworth**

ini **Charlesbridge**

To Barbara Davidson, for passing on those pet-loving genes; Emily Mitchell, for coming up with the purple-crested duchess monkey; my daughters, Jessica and Michelle, and their many beloved pets; and my husband, Steve, who makes it all possible—E. D. D.

To the Cookie Elves—M. C.

Published by Charlesbridge
85 Main Street
Watertown, MA 02472
(617) 926-0329
www.charlesbridge.com

Library of Congress Cataloging-in-Publication Data
Davidson, Ellen Dee, 1954-
    Princess Justina Albertina : a cautionary tale / Ellen Davidson ; illustrated by Michael Chesworth.
        p. cm.
    Summary: A spoiled, demanding young princess who sends her nanny to the far corners of the world in search of the perfect pet finally gets exactly what she deserves.
ISBN 978-1-57091-652-6 (reinforced for library use)
    [1. Pets—Fiction. 2. Princesses—Fiction. 3. Behavior—Fiction.] I. Chesworth, Michael, ill. II. Title.
PZ7.D28265Pri 2007
    [E]—dc22   2006009030

Printed in China
(hc) 10 9 8 7 6 5 4 3 2 1

Illustrations done in watercolor with colored pencil and gouache on Fabriano 140 lbs. hot press paper
Display type and text type set in Whoa Nelly and Obelisk
Color separations by Chroma Graphics, Singapore
Printed and bound by Jade Productions
Production supervision by Brian G. Walker
Designed by Diane M. Earley

PRINCESS JUSTINA ALBERTINA liked to have her own way. When she didn't get it, she got a funny look in her big green eyes and started to fuss. She caused a ruckus and a rumpus and a horrible hubbub. She made so much noise that it gave her nanny a headache.

So when Princess Justina Albertina said, "I WANT A PET!" her nanny went to the royal lagoon and scooped out a polka-dotted puffer fish.

Princess Justina Albertina watched her fish swim around inside a bowl. She tapped on the glass to get its attention. The fish swam faster and faster.

"This fish is no fun. I want a pet that notices me."

So her nanny roller-skated to town and bought a two-headed dog.

The dog licked Princess Justina Albertina all over her face. "Let's go for a walk," she said, climbing onto his back. The dog rolled over and played dead.

"This dog is lazy. I want a pet I can ride."

So her nanny climbed a rope to the enchanted forest and lured a unicorn with rose petals and songs.

Princess Justina Albertina made her unicorn trot and canter and gallop. Then she took it to the fence.

"Jump!"

The unicorn stopped. "Go! Leap! Dance! Pirouette!" she ordered, but the unicorn would not budge.

"This unicorn isn't listening to a thing I say.
I want a pet that listens!"

Her nanny sighed, but she grabbed her rubber boots and took a raft to Brazil. Then she waded up the Amazon until she found a talking toucan.

Princess Justina Albertina said, "Hello."
The toucan cocked her head to one side,
listening. Then she said, "Toucan."
"Say Justina Albertina!"
"Toucan."
"Justina Albertina! Justina Albertina!"
"Toucan. Toucan. Toucan."

"This toucan is too stupid to say my name.
I want a clever pet."

Her nanny frowned, but she took a magic carpet to Africa and soared over the jungle. At last, high in the leafy canopy, she found a purple-crested duchess monkey.

Her nanny shook her head, but she surfed the swells to Australia and brought back the famous flying kangaroo.

Princess Justina Albertina made a fist. "Let's try some kangaroo boxing."

The kangaroo flew into the sky. Princess Justina Albertina jumped up and let her fist fly. It smacked the kangaroo right in the face.

Her nanny ran over and pressed a cool
cloth to the kangaroo's face. "What have you
done, Princess?"

"This kangaroo is boring.
She can't even box. I want an
exciting pet."

Her nanny said, "Princess,
I think you have enough
pets already."

Princess Justina Albertina got a funny look in her big green eyes and started to fuss.

She caused a ruckus and a rumpus and a horrible hubbub. She made so much noise that it gave her nanny a headache.

So her nanny took a hot air balloon and went to the ends of the earth, searching the castles in the clouds, until she found a gryphon. The gryphon grimaced at being woken up, but he hopped about on his lion legs, flapped his heavy wings, and followed her home.

As soon as she
saw him, Princess
Justina Albertina
ran over and said,
"He's perfect. He's
exactly the pet
I want."

The gryphon opened his eagle beak and
swallowed Princess Justina Albertina in one gulp.

Then the gryphon burped and flew away.